Windows With Birds

Karen Ritz

BOYDS MILLS PRESS

HONESDALE, PENNSYLVANIA

For Daniel and his cat:

Houses are made
of brick and stone,
but homes are made
of love alone.

Text and illustrations copyright © 2010 by Karen Ritz

Boyds Mills Press, Inc.
815 Church Street
Honesdale, Pennsylvania 18431
Printed in the United States of America

Library of Congress Cataloging-in-Publication Data

Ritz, Karen.
  Windows with birds / written and illustrated by Karen Ritz. — 1st ed.
      p. cm.
  Summary: A cat adjusts to its new home in an apartment, high above the ground,
after living in a house.
  ISBN 978-1-59078-656-7 (hardcover : alk. paper)
  [1. Cats—Fiction. 2. Apartment houses—Fiction.] I. Title.
  PZ7.R519Wi 2010
  [E]—dc22
                                    2009019504

First edition
The text of this book is set in 18-point Goudy Old Style.
The illustrations are done in watercolor.

10 9 8 7 6 5 4 3 2

This was the house

that had windows with birds,

twenty-six stairs,

twenty-nine hiding places,

and one foolish mouse in the basement.

BOOKS ↑

This is the boy I pounced on
when he was quiet.

He filled my water dish, scratched me in just
the right places, and had friends I liked to play with.

I waited in a sunny spot
for him to come home.

The boy zipped me into his jacket
and brought me here.
Now, I shrink behind the couch and stare.

-FRAGILE-

He brings my water dish.
I am deep in a laundry basket
and won't come out, even when
he calls.

invisible up inside the box spring,
missing in the misery of a closet.

Meeoww! I wail, but he won't take me back to the old house.

He tries a mouse with a feather tail.
It smells of glue and dry grass.
In the dark hours, I chew it up
and leave it in a shoe.

The boy stops looking.
He is quiet.
His mom stays with him until he sleeps.

Me-ow.

In the dark hours,
I curl up when he stops tossing
and turning.

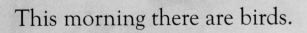

This morning there are birds.

I chase from window
to window,

I prowl along the sill
and hunt for where the boy
has moved my water dish.

up and down the furniture,
to ambush them in flight.

This is the home that has
windows with birds,

five perfect hiding places,

BOOKS

a promising new fish,

and the boy.

I wait in a sunny spot
for him to come home.